I0700283

Where the Warrior Lives

DALE ALLEN-ROWSE

Copyright © 2022 by Dale Allen-Rowse

All rights reserved. No part of this book may be used, reproduced, stored in a retrieval system, or transmitted in any form or by any means – electronic, mechanical, photocopy, recording, scanning, or other – except for brief quotes in critical reviews or articles without the prior written permission from the publisher.

Wolf Vision Publishing, LLC
P.O. Box 157
Mountain Center, California

www.DaleAllenRowse.com

ISBN (book): 979-8-9865306-4-2
ISBN (ebook): 979-8-9865306-5-9

Editor and Interior Design: Micah Schwader
www.inspiredlifepublications.com

Illustrations:
Sharon Sephton
www.earthgirl-art.org

DEDICATION

To all the queer individuals throughout history whose lives were cut short by toxic heteronormativity, righteousness, and hate. You deserved better, and I'm so sorry they couldn't see your perfection.

Table of Contents

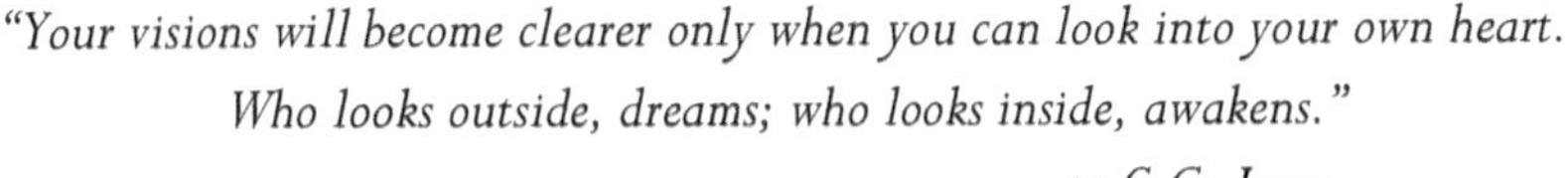

"Your visions will become clearer only when you can look into your own heart. Who looks outside, dreams; who looks inside, awakens."

~ C.G. Jung

Prologue

Melvin burst through the front door of the office building that housed his charges, panting like a maniac. He could barely hold the nearly dead tiny black child in his arms. He made his way through the children gathered in the foyer. "JOSEF!" He screamed up into the building. Josef spun around the corner, eyes wide.

"Herr," the junior officemate began, only to be cut off.

"Here," Melvin said, heaving the small boy's body into Josef's arms as the students began to close in to see what was happening. "Take him upstairs." The teacher then addressed the room. "Students who feel compelled to work in this healing, please follow." All stood stunned. Melvin then felt his ire and spoke directly. "IN MY PRESENCE," he said, clearly unsteadied by the stress of being covered in a child's blood. "You are never to question what you know. We DO NOT have time for this. Understood?!" he yelled. The class righted itself and burst into action, Josef leading the charge with the half-dead child in his arms. Melvin flew into his office to unearth his portal to his life behind the veil; adrenaline was the only thing keeping his mind in pure, mainlining focus.

Once his office door was secured behind him, Melvin cleared the floor to uncover the gate already humming in his ears. He quick-readied himself with his ceremonial robe, black facial markings prescribed by his faith, and a wolfen headdress to honor his family and lineage, the divine feminine. Watching himself adopt his truer form, Melvin involuntarily spun into a flashback—a reliving of his final moments with his Muttergöttin, Goddess Mother, as a child.

***

"We have prepared for this day, and it is here," Melvin remembered his mother saying. "You know enough to know where to start. Trust yourself. Trust the wisdom of our lineage. It will always serve your highest and best. When in doubt, listen there closest."

Those were the last words Melvin heard from his mother before he was given into the care of human parents from London while holding a black ceremonial robe. Arrangements had been made. Contracts had been signed. This was the final step. Melvin stepped into the room and grabbed a strange woman's hand to head to a strange home. He didn't look back as was instructed.

At fourteen years old, Melvin had no real comprehension of how life was about to change, but he understood why. He would see his family of origin again, but if he was to have a human experience that included a formal education, then this was the only way he could understand chemistry, physics, and the words spoken in the language of light.

Coming back to the present, Melvin exhaled into the mirror over the drawers in his office.

"You have to get this right," he leveled into his reflection. He turned and grabbed for his divining rod while onboarding spells.

It was go-time.

CHAPTER 1

TRUST

Once seated in the center of the Sol Invictus, his portal to the beyond, he flashed to Wereclair bright, then reverse swan-dived to part from his corporeal form; it bobbled with the departure.

Behind the veil, he leveled to a float, then cleared himself to blank where he inhabited stillness and vacated all truths. The sensation of unseen water wrapped his mind as he sought after the perfect question to most clearly define the answers he sought.

"I have done something that I do not understand the consequences of." His mind paused. He floated adrift, opening to trust. "I fear I may have performed unclean magic...." He exhaled the balance of the words, "Reveal to me how I might undo potential grave harm done to a child."

Melvin's mind reflected on what he knew about the intentions behind energy work. He knew that to inject Samuel with his Goddess Mother's protection, the incantation that awakens a child's inner warrior and then spring open the spell himself, was counter to the spell's intention. Melvin knew this. He could feel it in his guts, and to infect a boy with magic that may not burn clean is counter to everything his faith stood for.

He had to get this right, for he feared the mash-up of energetic counter-workings could be catastrophic to the child once the trap was sprung. He was all too familiar with how such 'accidents' of cross-grid melding could be. Some said he and his six siblings were such a hybrid. A ghastly cross-section of planes ever stuck in one reality. Melvin didn't know if that was folklore. However, he had heard it too often for it to now ring as false. Besides, it would explain why Wereclairs have no access to a power or spirit animal. Melvin often wondered if he and his wolf guide got weirded through a cross-plane collision. Regardless, it didn't matter. He was to this earth as he was supposed to be. That he held as personal truth above all else.

Settling the last molecules of resistance, Melvin repeated his ask into the ethers. "Reveal how I might undo potential grave harm to a child."

He slow floated in silence, but nothing was coming back. He checked again. In the still, again, nothing.

Feeling the pressure of the earth moment he was in, where his junior charges and officemate were dealing with a gravely wounded child, Melvin gave it two more long seconds before he called it quits. He understood that that's twice as long as needed for the universe to align to your ask once you do. If nothing was coming, then so be it. Melvin closed the space and flexed into a new vibe to chart a new course. He squeezed the Divining Rod to seek its information.

"Where to?" In one long second, he got the read and flew in its direction.

Minutes went by. Then more. Finally, after much longer than Melvin was comfortable, he stopped and questioned.

"I'm not understanding." He let himself clear to a still. "Today, I do not have time to go where you wish to go and...." He gained clarity. "Why is this taking longer than one long universal second?" He laughed hearing the words come out of his mouth. The ones that named his mistake. His misstep was immediately evident once he phrased his situation clearly.

"Gah!" he let fly as he chided himself for not seeing that his question was too loose and lacked specifics. "Undo potential harm?" He mocked himself. "The universe isn't that existential!"

Everywhere Melvin looked in the off-grid world was a cul-de-sac of returns — nothing was coming to him. He grabbed the next logical move.

"If nothing is coming to me...." He further emptied from himself to catch any breezes. "Do I need to go to it...?"

He felt himself ring with a 'yes' as he finished his sentence. Melvin was flustered, knowing he didn't have time for the journey. Not today.

"Fine," he said, uncoiling himself from the veil's web. "Another time," he said aloud, making it clear that he thought this would be easier than this was proving. His body hit a bounce with the reentry.

Upon regaining his senses, he, as always, felt the density of the earth. It was like a thud to the spirit that rang of drudgery and pain. He dimmed his eyes to yellow, then stood and undressed, avoiding his reflection in the mirror. The reflection that he only accepted because he had no other choice. His scrawny, teen-like frame was a lie to his mind, which was steeped in desire to bay at the moon and deliver casualties of ripped-throat death.

Melvin wiped the ceremonial markings from his face and kissed his tools before replacing them to the drawers. With weight gaining in his every move, Melvin returned to his earthly habit as he shed the last thoughts of himself. He hated that his incongruous vanity bothered him. He hated who he felt that made him because, in his heart, he knew he wasn't to serve himself. "Only spirit." He bowed. "Only the divine."

He then threw on his bloody human clothes and raced up the stairs carrying tools and weapons.

CHAPTER 2

TINDER AND SPARKS

"Josef!" Melvin yelled down the hall, searching frantically for Samuel. He knew the child was ultimately in good care, but that didn't mean there wasn't a mountain yet to climb to deal with what had transpired.

"In here," Josef cried from the dining room.

Melvin leaped for the sound of his junior's voice, and as he entered the dining area, he saw Samuel's near lifeless body on the table. He turned to address all who were present.

"Who has been called to heal?" Melvin said flatly, standing firm. Christian stepped forward. Her worry was obvious.

"Me," she said quietly.

"Me too?" Lukas said more as a question than a statement.

Silence then rang in the room.

"Who else has heard the call to heal?" The class could tell the seriousness of the moment. No one dared to breathe.

"Again, I ask. Anyone else?!" Melvin shot off.

The class stood in silence as one more voice made itself known. A voice that the teacher had been waiting to find itself. Lucien, the dark twin, stepped forward.

"I feel like...." the dark-spirited boy began.

Hearing his voice find truth, Melvin exhaled, celebrating the win. "Yes," the teacher encouraged, moving toward the boy whose pocket housed a severed human finger.

Lucien tried to finish his thought. "I don't understand...."

The teacher stopped the student. "I don't understand, yet," he corrected.

Lucien continued, "I don't understand yet, but maybe me too."

Melvin rushed to grab the child's face. "Yes. You too. You most of all." He brushed the boy's cheek saying, "Good job."

The mood in the space then flipped as Melvin, standing drenched in human blood, began barking orders.

"Christian and the twins, prepare to journey. Level up now. The rest of you…." He turned to face the terrified children. Seeing their fear, Melvin slowed himself, then reassured. "The rest of you," he repeated in a calmer tone, "go with Josef, please. Josef, I fear this may hamper our Christmas Eve celebration today." The moment's gravity hit Melvin's brain, making him double down on his focus. Melvin pulled Josef into a corner to conference in privacy.

"Samuel will be okay. He is under the care of Mother. He just needs time. Settle the children. Offer them lunch in the basement. See if you can get Herr Soliman. He deserves to know what has happened."

"How? — And we have Christmas Eve dinner planned," Josef tried, making his monumental efforts for the event known. "Can that still be on? Perhaps we invite him?" he hoped.

"Excellent plan. Get him here if possible. Tonight stands to be a special night indeed." Melvin pondered a promotion of sorts. "If you need help with the outside world, employ Johann and his power animal, Bumbgalla. For now, he is the muscle we have. I will be in the dining room with Christian and the twins looking after Samuel's care."

A tear of a man burdened with much then found its way to Josef's cheek. "He will be okay?"

"I promise," Melvin said, then he kissed his junior's forehead, but his junior didn't budge.

"I must know."

"What…?" Melvin hurried.

"Was a trap in Samuel sprung?" Josef asked while looking at the floor.

Melvin reviewed how best to answer that sticky question because he and Josef had had several conversations about releasing the boys' incantation of protection early, a thing counter to the magic's intention. A thing with unknown cross-grid implications.

"Indeed, it was, I'm afraid."

Josef looked into Melvin's face with horror. "Released by you?! No."

"It was the only option I had." The teacher then righted the student. "We will deal with the unknown consequences later. For now…" He hugged and held Josef, putting his pieces back together. "Let's celebrate his life as a Christmas miracle. How about that?" Melvin smiled at Josef. "Go. Lots to do."

Melvin closed the dining room's double doors and made ready the healing space.

"Christian. Close the blinds and darken the room. Twins, candles — about a dozen. Go!" Melvin addressed Samuel on the table, opening the space with rattled urgency. The boy was still breathing normally, and his heartbeat held steady. However, there was still no sign of consciousness. The teacher turned to ready himself, flying out of his clothes and into the ceremonial robe. He didn't have time to address long-established norms of nudity before others, besides what he was about to show his students would tower in their minds over any unexpected flesh of humankind.

Melvin adorned his face with his Nordic Paegan facial markings, grabbing for his headdress and divining y-shaped staff. When Christian, Lucien, and Lukas had completed their tasks, the teacher gathered them around.

"Come," he said as the room was rung with a new tone. "Sit on the table around Samuel. Christian at the feet, twins, on either side."

He then began the lesson by powering to his full Wereclair abilities. His eyes streaming light into the room, highlighting his physical transformation.

"What we have…," he began quietly, "we have to give." He turned to students in full wolf expression.

"Adopt your journeying state. Power up." Melvin watched with pride as his students demonstrated their gains. Christian flowed with healing feminine energy, her already growing hair shrouding her face. Melvin watched as she stepped behind the veil first.

"Excellent," the teacher offered as he saw Lukas also depart. He focused on the dark twin, Lucien, who seemed to be struggling.

"Lucien." The boy opened his eyes. "I'm sensing hesitation."

"Yes," the boy said.

"Why?"

Lucien's guts churned as he did his best to say what was in his heart. "I'm not sure."

"Of what, beloved?"

The child thought about it… "I guess I'm not sure of me."

Melvin pressed the question further. "You're not sure you'll do a good job, or is it that you think you're not right for this work?"

"Both, I guess."

Melvin dimmed his eyes so the dark-haired twin could more clearly see him. "I'm going to say a thing, and then you tell me what part of it is true."

"Okay."

"You indicated earlier that you felt you might not be right for healing work. You have also stated that your uniqueness makes you feel less than or sad."

"That's true, I guess."

"We need you to stand in your power, color, and truth. Do not shy away from who you are, although, please, after we're done here, you need to dispose of the finger."

The boy chuckled with embarrassment.

"Lucien. You are special and unique and will do great things—of that I'm sure. Your natural curiosity about the macabre greatly benefits all of us. You're the only one in the school with that gift. Just promise me that you won't judge your natural abilities until we discover, together, their potential and awesomeness." The teacher came close to make the final point.

"Promise me that?"

"Okay."

"Please…," Melvin stated into the room, leveling in glows. "Come. Lucien, join us in your journeying state." The boy blanked and left the room. The teacher followed.

CHAPTER 3

ARCING MATTER

Behind the veil, Melvin collected the students' wits. "What did I say before assisting Lucien?"

The blonde twin stepped up. "What we have, we have to give."

"Excellent." Melvin began. "So, answer the question. What do you have to give on this day to Samuel?"

"Healing," Christian offered with a smile.

"Yes, but say more," a comment that left a stump in the girl.

"Healing is…." Melvin prompted. However, not getting a response, he redirected. "What is your special way of healing that you bring to this table?" Another long silence. "Lucien?"

The dark twin rustled, "My uniqueness."

"Say more."

"My weirdness?"

Melvin laughed lightly. "And what's in that, that you have to give?" Still, silence rang in the students. Melvin tried another tac. "Go. Meet with your power animals and find out. I will return to the surface with Samuel. Go!"

Christian's horse was the first to arrive to ferry her off into the distance. Next was Lukas's magical glowing firefly and Lucien's massive black spider. The ogre-faced snapping beast scuttled about, making eerie ticking sounds. Lucien climbed on its back, and soon they too were gone.

Melvin threw himself back into the earthly realm, and reentering his body, he grabbed for Samuel's face. He dipped deep into the boy's subconscious to search for truths. After all, who was this tiny black eight-year-old boy? Melvin knew nothing of his being. He searched on, blanking himself to discover the child's vibe. Melvin exhaled and waited. Then slowly, as always happens, he started to feel a knowing off in the distance. Melvin prostrated himself to its truth, for universal intelligence speaks to those who grant newfound space while inhabiting a receiving expression. He emptied himself more and opened.

"Goddess Mother, grant me information," he said as it began to arrive in bass tones. Melvin reviewed what energies and entities live there. "Lower world," he said first, naming the signature's home. "Feels earthy — and...." He waited for more. The information came. "Musical." Melvin lit up with the realization. He knew that was enough to help the child find his mind's trailhead. He opened his eyes and refocused on a new get via a different route.

Melvin flashed his eyes as they closed while diving into the far side of his imagination—the portal to a divergent highway of messaging. He entered his mind's eye and ran from where he stood, into his body, down the portals and access points, and finally into Samuel's body as a tiny conscious seer. His mind's eye scanned the boy's insides for damage, then surveyed the beautiful work his mother had performed. He marveled at her mastery, her ability to bring love to an act of war. He headed back to the surface to reenter his vacated husk.

Melvin looked around the dim, quiet dining hall. The four of them held space for Samuel's body to heal. He looked at his students doing their work and felt a sense of pride in the lights being lit. He stepped behind the veil to conference.

"Come!" Melvin thundered into the beyond. In a long universal second, the children arrived. "What have you learned?" the teacher asked.

"May I ask a question?" Christian posed.

"Yes. Always," Melvin said. "Always ask. The more we openly discuss this process, the better."

"We came here to heal Samuel, yet all you have done is send us on errands to heal ourselves."

"Yes," Melvin confirmed. "Well done." He tapped the girl's nose with the tip of his finger.

"But that doesn't make sense…," Christian began.

"What was the first statement I made to this class?" Melvin said flatly.

Lukas cheered, "What we have, we have to give."

"Excellent — and if you arrive to a healing with broken parts within you…," he paused to punctuate the moment, "that's what you have to give. Is that what Samuel needs today?"

"No," Christian said sheepishly.

"So…," Melvin redirected. "What did you learn of your totem for healing work?"

"My totem stands for unity," Christian said, standing in her truth.

"How did it arrive?" Melvin asked.

The young woman thought about it. "As crystal blue…."

"Crystal blue what?"

"I'm not sure…." She searched her mind. "Light, I guess."

The teacher sought answers. "Was it conscious light?"

"Yes!" she said, recognizing a better way to language her understanding. "Yes. More like a light of intelligence."

"Excellent." Melvin clapped, trying to maintain a calm exterior. However, if what she said aligned with his understanding, this young woman would live to be an arc of force. It was awesome for Melvin to witness her unearth a new trailhead. "How about you, Lucien?"

The boy physically shored himself up. "It came to me as a nightmare." The boy was shaken.

"Okay," Melvin assured, bringing around his spider companion for warmth. "Here," he grounded them with calming energy. "Go on. How did your purpose in this work arrive?"

"It was…." Lucien started to cry softly, looking at his twin. "It was Pauline's last minute alive." Melvin recalled the news that the twins' sister somehow tragically died at a young age.

"You're okay. You're safe. Say what's true."

Lucien grabbed for Lukas and cried into him, saying, "She was there. I had her. She was okay…." He trailed off in tears.

"And then she was gone," his brother finished for him.

"And then she was gone. I couldn't let her go. I had to go after her, but that man stopped me from diving under the ice."

"I know," Lukas soothed

"I have to be there for her, and I will forsake all else to do so. It was my fault." The boy plunged into a wail of despair that the teacher stepped in to silence. Melvin reached into Lucien's way and dimmed a light until the boy fell asleep. To do otherwise seemed unnecessarily cruel.

Melvin turned to address Lukas and his firefly. "And what of you? What have you learned?"

"My totem for this work arrived as a sensation of, almost… I guess it's the feeling of childhood wonder. Isn't that what you called it?"

Melvin's mind was blown hearing this story. If this child's totem for healing work was childhood wonder, which is the first step out of the egoic mind toward heart-based consciousness, then this would be interesting indeed. "How did it arrive?"

"As a close-up view of my spirit animal's abdomen. Like a… a cold light."

The portal being named was thrilling to Melvin. "Excellent." He faced all three and named the work before the students. "So I ask again. What do you have to give to Samuel?"

"I do not understand how unity can heal this child," Christian said.

"How was this child wounded? Search there. If unity on earth existed, would this tiny child have been shot in the back?" Melvin stooped to wake Lucien. "What do you have to give to Samuel today?"

Rousing himself right, the dark twin eventually offered, "Lightness in the dark."

"You are the bravest of all, aren't you?" Melvin said, smiling. "It takes a special being to hold and create spaces at night. It is only by the powers of the dark that there is light. Do you understand that?"

"Yes."

"What you witnessed is a special calling, not for the weak."

"I understand."

"And whenever you feel frightened or overwhelmed, think of your sister and tell her that you will always be there for people like her. Hold her in the in-between and bring love and light to the darkness."

A tear fell from the boy's eye as he nodded in agreement.

"And you, Lukas? What is your answer?"

"My answer is the same. To bring light to the dark."

"But then, how is what you're bringing to Samuel different or unique from your brother?"

"Well...," the teen pondered, "I guess where Lucien heads into the darkness, I head into the light."

"Most excellent." Melvin clapped. "Say more."

"Not sure."

"Look closer," the teacher encouraged. "I think there's more for you in there."

"Look closer? Into the bioluminescence?"

"Stop questioning and open yourself to the answer."

Lukas blanked himself as they had practiced, and they all waited for his realization. "There's… It's almost microscopic. Like cells."

"And…?" Melvin sought.

"And it's not of this earth."

"Say more," Melvin pressed

"It's like a link."

"Good. Yes. Like a link. At least we know where to begin and now what to look for. That was excellent. So what do you have to offer Samuel?"

"Not sure."

"Meet him where he is. Find the path to his trust through childhood wonder. How does that sound as a start?"

"Very excellent." Lukas laughed.

"Good." Melvin smiled. "Time to head back, however, before we leave." He opened his feelers to maximum capacity and then listened. "I feel like there is calling between the three of you, not just the twins being the duality of darkness and light." He double-checked how what he just said felt. He sensed no lies; it rang as true within him. The teacher continued, "It feels like a trinity here, and I encourage you to explore what I'm sensing. Christian, since your charge is unity, I ask that you lead."

She nodded in agreement as they stepped back into the dining room and opened their eyes.

CHAPTER 4

RIVER'S RUN

Seated upon the dining table, Melvin spoke directly. "Now demonstrate what you have to give. Christian, find the trinity but remain here. We will send for you in time."

"Understood." She nodded.

Melvin kissed Samuel's forehead, leaped from the table, and returned to his bloody human clothes—for to walk the halls in his ceremonial garb would be heresy—and then left the room searching for Josef.

Turning the corner, Melvin ran into Fritz in the hall.

"Have you seen Josef?"

"He's in the basement setting something up."

"Excellent," Melvin said, then flew down the stairs.

"Josef!" he yelled, not yet reaching the basement landing.

"Herr."

The two men met just feet from the stairs. "Any word of Herr Soliman?"

"Yes. He understands his child is here and in good care. He is collecting a few things because I told him he might be with us as needed. Certainly, until Samuel is well."

"Are you still able to manage Christmas Eve dinner?"

"Oh yes!" Josef clapped gayly. "Shall be very special indeed."

"With you in charge, dear one." He moved in to hug his junior. "I have no doubt." Melvin redirected. "I have verified Samuel's wounds — while bad, he will live. When Herr Soliman arrives, I must speak with him."

"I will see to it," Josef assured.

Melvin kissed the young man's head and said, "Thank you." He rushed to his office to update his long-departed lover, Nikolai Tesla. The science to his magic.

Dearest Nikolai,

I fear we are in real trouble.

Where do I even begin to relay all that has happened? Know that we stand on shifting sands and that I have been seen and named by authorities while whisking away a child under the Government's control. It was only by the graces of our informant at the hospital, Herr Soliman, the only black family in town, that we found out. He has been a loyal supporter of our cause. Somehow the policing forces captured his son and scheduled him for their 'Ausegebesser,' lobotomy mending. It makes no sense to one's mind. The boy is eight years old! What justification can they possibly take for operating on an infant without their consent?!

The spell of 'der Zauberspruch' had to be used to save the boy's life. However, I installed the 'Det store vesenet' The Great Becoming and then sprung it to life within the child. This is very much counter to the spell's intention. At this time, we do not know what this might mean for the boy's future. Only time will tell.

The good news is that I have ended the Church & Government program. I do hope permanently. It was certain justice I had to take into my own hands. May I find peace from the decision. These things are never easy, and I regret to inform you that we have lost another twenty-seven young men who we were too late to save from surgically altered minds. They will live on as if zombies were real and made. Of the twenty-seven we lost, four were not children we knew. I honestly don't know the value of keeping 'the register' in this amount of chaos.

Johann continues to learn how to be with Bumbgalla, his Gorilla power animal, which I hope will be beneficial to Samuel.

The other students who live permanently in your building are thriving. Christian, the only female of the group, is transitioning beautifully into a powerful woman. Her thurst for justice is remarkable, but her take on justice is from a point of view that awes me. She seems moved by the layer above earthly justice — the justice that strives for a higher place, a place of unity. The arc of justice blares bright in this one, and I cannot wait to see who she becomes.

The Twins are discovering their balance in this work, with Lucien finding himself and gaining in his personal belief. Lukas has shown himself more this week as well. He has a lightness to him that I'm curious about. Having heard how their sister died, I fear the boy's buoyancy has been hyped within himself to counter the depths of his brother's despair. Many questions remain unanswered.

The lovers inspire us all with their open displays of affection. A thing most of us never thought we could ever even see, let alone hold as a dream for ourselves. Felix is bombastic at times, and Jakob, we can tell, is gunning for a house and a white picket fence. It's truly a delight to see love in our midst.

Then lastly, Matteo is our curious one. He reads up on everything. Kindly send books that might ignite his curiosity. He seems keen on stories of alien intelligence, solving problems in creative ways and mysteries.

Then to request again, and I'm certain it's underway. However, I have not received the forged medical degree documentation for myself nor the plans for the school in upstate New York. With things going here as they are, I am keen to stay up on as much as possible. Plus, I fear the authorities will be knocking any day.

In closing, Merry Christmas, beloved. It is very hard some days to stay strong, but I use my imagination to dream of the days yet to come where we can be together and grow a free school for all, the understood and the not understood. We deserve better than to be hunted as freaks.

Josef is doing well and has made fantastic feasts for the children and Herr Soliman, who will join us until his son is well enough to go home. It shall be a beautiful evening. Much to celebrate.

I love you more than words can express.
Very truly yours,

Melvin

Chapter 5

Chances

"Herr Soliman has arrived," Josef said, peeking into Melvin's office.

"Excellent. Thank you — and please put this letter to Herr Tesla with the outgoing post," Melvin said, handing his junior the letter.

"Herr Soliman," Melvin said, entering the old office building's foyer. "We're so glad you can be with us." Realizing he didn't know if more family members would be joining, he sought, "Anyone else in the family that might need assistance at this time?"

The black man shuffled in toward Melvin. He was easily twice Melvin's twenty-four years. "It's just me...." His spirit seemed beat. "And Samuel. Please take me to him."

"Of course," Melvin assured, taking the man up the stairs.

"Christian, Lukas, Lucien... this is Samuel's father," Melvin said, opening the double doors. "Please leave us. Send in Johann." His charges showed reverence to Herr Soliman and his hour of need.

"Come. Please. Sit." Melvin indicated to a chair next to Samuel, who remained unconscious on the table.

The father rushed to grab at his son, worry his only resonance. "Samuel!"

After Herr Soliman had a chance to regain himself, Melvin beat to the heart of the matter. "What do you know of why we seek information on these boys?"

"From the look of them as a gaggle," the man indicated to the space beyond the dining room doors. "You want to help the effeminate."

Melvin was taken aback at how succinctly the situation was being read. "Excellent. We have an understanding. So…." Melvin skirted around the flounce of the topic, "Does this mean…?" he redirected. Asking the man directly if his son was displaying such traits felt incorrect. "Tell me about Samuel."

Herr Soliman smiled and looked at his tiny perfect face, now asleep for too long. "He is a funny boy. Oh, he makes me crack up!" The man let out a memory that sounded like a laugh. "He loves to play percussion… AND BASS!"

"How amazing," Melvin wondered.

"Has to stand on a stool — but for a child of his size, he can make it ring!" Smiles and warmth were exchanged between the two men.

"There's something else," Melvin offered quietly, bringing the space to a new tone.

"Oh?" Herr Soliman questioned. "About what?"

"It's about how I was able to save Samuel's life."

"Your boy said it was a bullet…." Herr Soliman pleaded. He continued, "in his back."

"Indeed, it was." Melvin regrouped, "It should have been fatal, but I was able to save him." Herr Soliman didn't move, so Melvin continued. "What do you think of people having special abilities."

"What do you mean?" the senior man asked, confused. A light knock was heard on the double doors.

"Johann. Come!" Melvin yelled to be heard by the child.

The doors opened, and a child of twelve with an eerie stare stood awaiting direction.

"Come. Come," the teacher encouraged the student into the conference. He made the introductions. "Herr, this is Johann. He is our upperclassman for now and walks with the same spirit as Samuel."

"What? I don't understand."

"As we began discussing, what do you think of humans with special abilities."

"Physical abilities?"

"Well… yes — and no," he said, taking the senior's hand while allowing his eyes to return their natural glow. "It's more how some have access to adjust the physical through the spiritual. The unseen affecting the seen."

Herr Soliman gathered Melvin to the corner of the room with a fluster and a hurry, a move that was a first for the teacher. Normally, when he reveals himself in this manner, the response is disbelief, not run to the corner and conference.

"This is not something to be done in this country. It is not safe. It is why I live amongst these unevolved white men." Melvin couldn't help but let go of a light laugh of relief over the man's reaction to his magic.

"Certainly, in Nigeria, we have our own such people."

"Yes," Melvin cheered. "Tell me of them."

"This is not safe to discuss here."

The teacher cut to serious. "And yet we must. Your child's life has been altered by it, and…." Melvin shoulder-checked the dark room. "And it now lives within him." Melvin hung his head. "It is what I had do to save his life."

This comment moved the older man. He embraced Melvin saying, "Thank you."

"Tell me of your healers. I want to know, but first, we must tend to Samuel. It is why I have brought Johann because his magic and inner warrior have already been brought to life. We may use him as an example so you might know what to expect."

"Understood," Herr Soliman said. "Show me. I can face this without fear if it means saving my boy's life."

"Come," Melvin said, then led them to sit with Herr Soliman on his left, Johann on his right, and he at the head. They joined hands.

Melvin leveled to Wereclair bright as Johann followed. His dark green eyes eerily watched the room with primate consciousness.

"Herr Soliman. In our efforts to save these non-conforming men, we have called upon the diety, The Great White Wolf, The Divine Feminine on earth. How do you recognize such a being in your faith or practice?"

"My family is of the Vodun faith." Melvin was delighted to hear more.

"Yes...? Tell me of it."

"We recognize the intelligence in our ancestors and believe the dead are still in our family." He paused, and a new sadness found its way to his face. "I think it is why they vilify us so."

"Because your elders still walk with you?"

"I do not believe they see it that way. They see our relationship with death as wicked, but they simply don't understand our ways."

Melvin exhaled. "You may be correct. I, too, leverage the wisdom from our elders."

Herr Soliman was genuinely curious. Melvin dimmed his eyes to speak more closely. "And it is from that source energy that your son has been altered. He now holds the energy, as does Johann." The boy's eyes dimly glowed deep emerald green. "Do you understand, sir? This is not evil. This will not harm him but greatly advance what was already there."

"Are you one of them?" the man asked, making Melvin laugh.

"Oh, no. Not the same thing. I'm more of a cross-section of spirits or entities, whereas Samuel's gifts will simply be heightened by his already existing human gifts. We do not know to what extent." He then turned to his student while continuing to speak to Herr Soliman.

"In my spiritual practice, we leverage what is. What already exists. Build on what nature has available to us. This includes a personal tour guide to the universe. In Johann's case, his guide is from the Primate Nation. A gorilla named Bumbgalla. They have a special connection and deep love for one another. They run and play and learn in the off-grid planes for now, but eventually, they will be skilled enough to leverage these lessons in the physical world. Johann, please bring Bumbgalla to the veil's curtain." Within a long universal second, Bumbgalla appeared as a shimmering apparition. "Do not bring him forward to this plane."

Melvin focused on Herr Soliman. "Is there anything you wish to ask?"

"Will he still be my boy? Will he still be himself?" he cried.

"Most certainly. However, he may develop a slight obsession with meditating. Other than that, I foresee no problems." The last bit Melvin heard was too hopeful to be believable. "Do you want us to leave you with him?"

"Thank you."

"Johann. Come." Melvin left the space with the small boy to check on Josef's Christmas Eve feast.

CHAPTER 6

ALACRITY

"Josef!" Melvin yelled into the upstairs hall.

"In the basement," Felix offered.

"Again?"

"Still."

"Ah." Melvin hurried, curious to see what his charge was up to. Arriving at the blast-proof concrete basement, Melvin checked the lights. "Gah!" As per usual, it would be dark, lit only by candles.

"Oh, no need." Josef scampered over. "I have it all set with…." He took Melvin by the sleeve and drew him across the floor. "These!" he ta-dah'd.

Melvin took in the amazing chandeliers draped in evergreens, berries, fruits, and candles. "You, sir, never fail to amaze."

"Here. Help me get them lit and strung up."

The men set about with the decor of the space, Melvin lending speed to set things right.

The room was almost complete when four in the afternoon was rounding the clock, and the sun had begun its set. "Call the students. Tonight, we feast and there indeed is much to celebrate." A thing that failed to ring with unbridled delight because one in attendance still failed to be conscious. Melvin fake-pepped the best he could. "I shall collect Samuel and his father. Let's be seated by 5:00. However, I wish to begin our meal in conference with the children."

"I will make it so." Josef nodded, adding the final touches to the tablescape.

"Bumbgalla's feeding trough. Where is it?"

"By the stairs," Josef nosed toward it. "Why?"

"Just make do with what we have so all can attend this Christmas Eve's celebration night."

As the sun slipped behind the horizon, the excitement within the building grew. Candles were lit, and a few special items were wrapped. It was as if the air itself was ionized with joy.

Melvin ran upstairs to collect Samuel and call everyone to supper. "Come on! Josef has everything set. It's really amazing," Melvin encouraged as everyone ran and yelled with good cheer.

Once everyone settled into the dark gymnasium, a hush fell over them. Before them, the most beautiful party they had ever been invited to attend. In his undying way, Josef had seen to every last detail and painted delight into every corner of the room. Its bohemian simplicity only added to its wholesomeness. The children took it in with delight. Down the length of the table, chandeliers were hung from the ceiling made from discarded old wagon wheels that Josef had turned on their side, and there were special treats that could be smelled in the air. The table was a terrific delight; a festival of berry boughs, candelabras, packaged gifts, and mismatched finery.

Melvin made his way through the room carrying Samuel. Herr Solimann followed. Next to the head of the table, Melvin had placed Bumbgalla's trough, which was now outfitted as a makeshift bed. Melvin placed the child on the sheets, and the world felt restored as this tiny child of color, the son of Herr Soliman, slept in their rightful place at the head of the table.

"Please sit," Melvin said. He looked across to his dependable charge Josef and spoke. "We can never lose sight of our blessings. Samuel will recover." The room celebrated with cheers. "But the road ahead is unknown. Allow me to recount what transpired this morning after Herr Soliman arrived with the horrible news that the surgeries have resumed and that they had his son." Melvin struck a sullen tone. "We were able to save Samuel, but unfortunately, we were too late to save twenty-seven who were surgically removed from their minds." A hush fell over the room. "These are very serious times for us, the non-conforming. We cannot lose sight of that." Melvin regrouped. "I have ended the program at the hospital, but that doesn't mean that the minds who put it into action have also been halted. I have done what I can to administer fear to cease their efforts. This is why." He punctuated into the air. "This is why our work is so serious. Allow me to explain." He paused to refocus and clarify the many weeks of work. "It may seem we are only having you work on yourselves, developing a spiritual practice. Working behind the veil. Meditating to find the quiet mind. But this is how we take it all down. This work is what ends with children being shot in the back." He turned with concern to the little child.

"Samuel's trap has been sprung. He now lives with Det store vesenet," he said in his Norwegian native tongue. "It means, 'The Great Becoming.' His power animal did become present. However, Samuel began to lose consciousness the moment it did. I can report it appears to be a pachyderm of tremendous size."

A rumble of murmurs went around the room as Melvin continued, "We do not know how this will affect Samuel as we haven't been able to instruct him on managing such a transformation. Therefore, we must keep him down here in the gymnasium if he becomes conscious and unleashes such a beast.

Johann." The steely twelve-year-old looked over, already understanding what was coming next.

"On it," the preteen smirked, making Melvin laugh and recognize the kid was finding his chops.

Good for you, kid, Melvin thought. *Nice to see.*

"Thank you," Melvin said.

"Let's eat!" Josef yelled, making everyone cheer.

The evening was festive and divine. They ate and laughed and told grand stories, some of which were, in fact, true.

After the meal, Josef had a gift for each student. Matteo was given books. Christian was given an old fiddle that Josef negotiated for some sewing work. He had overheard her once saying that she knew how to play.

Johann was given a ceremonial robe, and the twins both received outdoor prayer lanterns that ferry off dreams and wishes. Felix received a fashionable shirt that Josef sewed, and Jakob was gifted lessons to learn how to cook.

Melvin had taken care of Samuel and Herr Soliman's gift.

"For you," Melvin began, "the totem of friendship from my people." Herr Soliman opened the box.

"A sigel?" he asked, inspecting the medallion on a chain.

"It is a symbol of luck. For me, what I have, I have to give."

"And you have luck to give?"

Melvin thought on it, smiled, and then responded, "Luck is like an opportunity — it can only be seen by those who believe it is there."

"Indeed." Herr Soliman smiled.

Melvin turned to Samuel. "For you, beloved," he said, laying a wreath of blessings and healing incense at the child's feet. "The one who has given so much, I ask that you forgive a world that has failed you. I am so sorry." Melvin continued fighting back the tears. "You didn't deserve this, and we will make it up to you." He quietly indicated to the students. "We all will make it up to you. I know you didn't ask to be born into this war. None of us were, yet here we are. So what do we do?" Melvin hung his heavy head in the presence of a senior and repeated, "What do we do?"

Herr Soliman took Melvin's hand, responding, "We make good trouble."

CHAPTER 7

ALLAYING NÖEL

Melvin awoke in his office, as had become habit. He looked out the window into the morning light and realized a skiff of snow had been delivered in the night. Its frozen edges lended the morning air prisms of possibilities for the day.

He stirred himself awake and, knowing it would be a long day, thought it best if he observed some self-care first. He undressed, then stepped into his ceremonial gown, readied his facial markings, and grabbed for the headdress. He cleared the floor to reveal the Sol Invictus while onboarding spells.

Grabbing his Divining Rod, he flung his soul backward to depart from his earthbound thickness. Behind the veil, he flew to his favorite yet most hated place, Nikolai's room in America. A space he would haunt when his mind could bear to only see him and be allowed nothing more. It was a queer crush of the heart that both killed his spirit yet watered him.

Melvin lowered himself beside Nikolai's bed, and a tear dropped as he managed, "Merry Christmas, my love."

That was all his heart could take; he flew back into his body with a thud. Melvin opened his eyes and cried, making a mess of his makeup. "Shit." Melvin laughed while crying. He retrieved a towel and made an effort to restore his earthly lie. There was a knock at the door.

"I figured you'd still be here," Josef said through a cracked door. "Breakfast is ready."

"Thank you, Josef. What would we do without you?"

"Starve and be sad." Josef offered a plain response.

"Indeed." Melvin chuckled. "Be right there."

Upstairs, there was a fair amount of boys being girls, and such. The excitement of the celebratory day very much alive in their hearts.

"Come," Josef said, collecting them as Melvin arrived at the head of the table. The students eventually arrived and settled. Melvin stood to address the room.

"Samuel remains in good care. Herr Soliman is with him in the basement. We will see he is well taken care of." He nodded in Josef's direction, who winked an 'already on it' in response. "Very good." Melvin laughed to himself. "Today, on this Christmas Day, we will still have class." The room deflated into a groan. "Listen, listen...." Melvin smiled, demonstrating he was in on the joke. "You're going to like this one." A few more moans went around, making Melvin draw the class's attention. "What do we do when we're presented with something new?"

There was silence, then Johann spoke up and said, "Apparently groan."

This comment from this normally near-mute child was enough to throw the entire room into gales of laughter that lasted until sides were split.

"Yes!" Melvin pepped. "Exactly...." He laughed on, then recovered. "But what's the rule? What are we supposed to do when presented with new information? Johann?"

"Remain in curiosity."

"Thank you — excellent!" He cheered on, "Eat! But class at 9:00 in here. Not downstairs." The room was already bursting with movement and plates being passed. Melvin eventually gave up and joined in the revelry.

The Christmas morning breakfast was alive with the student's laughter and tales. Matteo told of a ship adventure he was on in his latest novel. Josef was his always boisterous self, and the meal was enjoyed by all that attended.

As the morning lazed on, the lounging group slow-gathered for class.

"Come!" Melvin snapped. "Sit. Johann, across. Twins on my left, Christian on my right." The young people scuttled into place at the table. "Good." The room eventually came to a halt, with Jakob and Felix being the last to tuck in.

"All set, sir," Josef said quietly, closing the dining hall double doors.

"Thank you, Josef. Please...." He indicated his rightful spot at the table.

"On this Christmas morning, we are blessed." Smiles went around the room. "We have so much that we have much to give. Do we not?" Melvin hailed. "So what is it you have to give this Christmas?" A seriousness found its way into the space. "What's in here?" Melvin pointed into his chest. "Because today's lesson, on this beautiful day, is based on what gifts we have to give. So!" he redirected lightly. "What do you have to give today? What's its tone?" Melvin stood and walked the perimeter of the table. "We started this with Christian and the twins in their healing work with Samuel, using our spirit guide to show us what we need to see and know. I'd like to expand this lesson to include everyone. Christian. How was that experience for you yesterday?"

She moved some of her long hair behind her ear, saying, "There's not much to do. That surprised me."

"Say more about that," the teacher encouraged.

"It's that they are the guides. They took us right where we needed to go. It was surprisingly easy."

"Like they were guiding you?" Melvin teased.

She laughed, "Yes. Exactly."

"What was the energy signature of your guide?"

"He's a sleek horse. He…." She thought harder for the right words. "He's caring."

"He exudes love."

"Yes. It's hard to describe."

"And where did your guide take you, and where did you go?" Melvin pressed.

"It was a well."

"In the ground?"

"Yes — and when I peered into it, I saw this crystal blue light that shimmered with information."

"The language in light," Melvin said, recounting the moment he first heard those words spoken by a stranger who would, in time, become his love. "Go on…," he encouraged the young woman. "Say more."

"It looked like light, but somehow it didn't feel like light. It felt like intelligence," she continued.

Mouths could be heard dropping open.

"For truth!?" Matteo countered energetically.

"Matteo. Hush."

"I just want to know…," the curly boy smarted. "Geez."

The room refocused on Christian, who continued. "It somehow let me know that my totem for this work is unity."

"So you feel called to the realm of healing work from the arc of unity."

She smiled despite herself, recognizing the bigness of the bell that was just rung. "Wow."

"Wow, indeed," Melvin reassured. "Lucien? How about you? Tell us of your journey with your guide."

"Mine arrived as trauma."

"Excellent," Melvin encouraged. "Say more about the value you were able to receive from your trauma. What learning was there for you? What do you now know that you didn't previously? Go on...."

The boy found a twist in him that wouldn't quit as he managed, "My guide is a spider...." He looked around the room for judgment but, finding none, he continued. "His name is Cleaver."

The room erupted with laughter. His twin asked, "You named him?"

"Lukas! What do you know of your brother's journey?! Nothing," he scolded, bringing the room to a new silence. "Let me ask you." He redirected to the dark white boy. "Lucien. Did you name him, or did he tell you his name?"

"He told me his name," the boy said sadly, making the teacher turn to the other students, ensuring they all got 'the look.'

"Do we have an understanding?" Melvin asked pointedly as halfhearted grumbles again met the air. He relaunched his discovery. "What was your totem for this work?"

"My totem was found in the last minute of my sister's life. She slipped from my hands to her death. My totem is...." he questioned in an aside, "It's psychopomp work." He looked to the teacher, who, with a smile, confirmed he had said it correctly. "And it was found through the undying love I have for her."

The teacher drove the point further. "Through this work and gaining insight into your calling, do you hold your trauma differently?"

"Not certain I understand," Lucien said.

"Is there now newfound value to your trauma?"

The boy thought on it. "I guess… in a way."

"What have you learned there that you wouldn't trade for anything?" Melvin pressed.

"I know myself differently. It's like the edges of me were stretched. I know much greater love, but I also know much deeper sadness."

"Repeat after me," Melvin said into the boy's eyes. "And for that, I am blessed."

"And for that, I am blessed," he repeated.

"Lukas? Tell us of your experience."

"My firefly showed me his abdomen, which contains bioluminescence. It didn't make perfect sense, but she told me it was a link. I don't understand it yet."

Melvin reseated himself at the head of the table in a serious tone. "We are still very much in the early stages of getting acquainted with our spirit guides, with the exception of Johann. He has gained what we hope you too will master." Melvin closed his eyes and made his ceremonial prayer fists to enter himself. "In our work, there are three mind merges," he clarified in a serious tone. "You have been enjoying, playing, and getting familiar with the realm below these three merged planes; a child's playground of imagination, nothing more. However, that is the trailhead that every great warrior must first pass." He paused to gather the tension. "Where does the warrior live?" Johann lit the room with impossibly dark green light waves. The teacher followed with similar resonance in white, saying to the class, "I'll meet you there. Go."

CHAPTER 8

CHRISTMAS PUNCH

The students were well into their lesson when there was a knock on the door. However, with class in session and Herr Soliman and Samuel in the concrete basement, no one heard its intrusive Christmas Day rap. A note was slipped under the door.

"Herr Vaughn?" Matteo questioned.

"Yes?" Melvin responded, closing the dining room from class.

"There's a note here on the floor."

Melvin fetched it and spilled its guts, reading:

> *We know who and what you are.*
> *Return my son and leave immediately,*
> Commettant Maier

There was only one place Melvin could solve this. He headed for the Sol Invictus.

Within seconds, he had the floor clear as the star's consciousness flared and materialized. Melvin opened his mind to its understanding while simultaneously onboarding spells. "The Path Home." He felt its gain. "Centering Truth… Clarity Chant…" They ping-ponged within him. "Divining Rod." He linked to its know, which was akin to a fisheye lens, in terms of what he could receive from beyond him. It was the extra inch of understanding he could get from the y-shaped branch while also providing greater depth of field in his off-grid vision.

Melvin readied his corporeal form and then seated himself in the knowledge of the star. He flicked his moonbeams to the max, then blanked himself for the ride.

He was in.

First door: Bodhate/Budh. "Go Melvin boy," he cheered. Second door: Swapna. His easy vibe was playing on the new plane. He hit the thrusters. BOOM! — the breaking of barriers broke as things atomized around him anew. He was in. "GO! GO!" Melvin slow-rolled while gaining speed and leveling in focus. Third door: Shabdkosh. Melvin flexed his outer shell. BOOM! He was through. On and on, Melvin pushed his speed out of frustration at a world so hellbent on erasing human expression. Fourth door: Khandbahale... Whoosh!!! He flew through it for the first time, and the spray of exaltation from the beyond gave him what he needed in his moment of need. He named the get. "Fourth door, Khandbahale." A thing he was only able to best from the lens of teaching because, in that inhabitance, he was a teacher in name only. His truer vibration when inside the bubble of a class was a student.

Melvin recalled the moment with Johann and how he was humbled to receive such a massive understanding from such a tiny child. He let the experience roll through him as he slowed to a float. He wasn't up for the effort of trying Door Five, so best to simply enjoy the victory that was just scored. He smiled, knowing he had done what, at one time, seemed impossible. He leaned into Self-Honor as was the way of his people. He held a reverence in the moment that named his gratitude. A special place found at the intersection of self-knowledge and self-care, a thing which, by extension, honors the intelligence of all.

Melvin emptied from himself, his mind's sails adjusting to universal winds. He floated on, allowing everything to be without his energetic interruption. The place where the observer no longer affects the observed.

He slowed. Then slowed some more. He connected and then dialed to 73 kilometers per second per megaparsec (plus or minus one). He zeroed to her frequency, not daring to breathe, allowing creation to be as it sees itself.

He detected a snag in the web and awaited its arrival.

"Son." It was his mother, The Divine Feminine, arriving.

Melvin bowed, suddenly breathing heavy. "Mother."

"Stand," she thundered. Melvin arrived to meet her gaze; his eyes peeled like peaches. She continued, "Is it true?" Melvin's guts hit the brakes, making him feel a death inside. Again, he knew his mistake before she even named it. He had failed. Again.

"Is my child a murderer?" The metal in her voice was piercing.

Melvin didn't move.

"SPEAK," she commanded. "And only answer the question at hand, for we are not judged by our reasons but rather by our actions." She paused, then drove home the point. "Måne." She addressed his birth name, meaning 'Moon' in Norweigein. "It can never be about reasons. It can never be about justice or justifications. To hold those things above what is loving or compassionate is counter to our ways." She gave the moment some time. "This fight in you. It is how you fail. That is the light that must be distinguished. You will never accomplish what's needed until you can gain that tone. You have learned and adopted lies that you co-opt for more of the same. Violence served as justice, and bigotry served as morality. There can be no winning from this vibration. Since you were already censured, your punishment now is to be...." She paused before letting the final sentence be said, "You are cast out. Goodbye son. I wish you well, but you are no longer welcome in our homeland. Punishment for returning will be death."

With that, she was gone, and Melvin cratered into himself, feeling every ounce of shame imaginable. He wasn't sure he had done right, but it felt right. It felt justified.

While still slow floating in the ethers, a tendril snagged a new know. He verbalized the get. "Hate doesn't feel like hate on the inside — it feels like righteousness."

The tone of the message thunderstruck Melvin into a new tone: regret. He was pained with the realization, fighting to stay open to what was, knowing that to fight anything is to fight our own alignment. He centered, allowing messages to wash over him. A new tone then came in. It rang like his last journey. He knew this pull! It was the one that wouldn't obey 'universal time' or, as more accurately described, the complete abolishment of the time concept. The pull that failed to yield or materialize along the one long universal second rule: the amount of time needed for the universe to align to what the individual is pinging with.

"Why is this new understanding not materializing like normal?" he wondered, tugging at its seams. "What are you made of?" He adopted curiosity and set to mentally dismantle the thing to see what he could gain.

"Doesn't recognize the traditional concept of time, as I understand it," Melvin first proffered, jumping next to other attributes. "Feels…." He searched for what was true. "Distant. Not… menacing. I'm not getting that vibration."

Knowing he didn't have much time, Melvin packed away his latest understandings to crunch through later. However, before his departure, he had one final errand. An ask.

"Benevolent allies. Ancestors. What do I need to know?" He then adopted his receiving state and awaited the call. It came back as "Avoid fear. It is too costly."

Hearing that this was the response, Melvin released the stillness within while not having any clue as to how he could even manage such a thing. How does one win a war while never being in fear? "What's the opposite of fear? Love," he questioned then answered himself. "How does one win a war while in a state of love?" His head spun, and he headed back to the surface of his mind.

After returning to his body, Melvin stood and walked over to the mirror above the drawers in his office. He took off his lupine headdress and undressed. He wiped off his ceremonial marking, feeling the slough of all the impossible things that now filled his mind.

Grabbing for his pants and earth clothes, he reviewed his journey. It wasn't much, but at least he had some direction from beyond him, whether he currently understood it or not.

CHAPTER 9

BREAKING TWILIGHT

The evening celebrations were winding to a close, and Melvin and Josef saw the students to bed. They cleaned up some of the spaces, and as Melvin was about to call it a night, Josef walked in holding a bottle of champagne and two glasses.

"Dare to go sit on the roof and bay at the moon?"

Melvin laughed in spite of himself. "Yes, to the sitting part. No, to the baying. I'm now certain we're being watched."

"No more problems for the rest of the day. How about that?" Josef suggested.

"Dear sir, you truly are a friend — agreed." Melvin smiled.

"Ex-cell-ent," Josef sang, heading up the stairs.

Once settled under the moon, Melvin noticed the clarity of the night and how the air seemed thinner than normal. They exhaled visible breath in the cold night, and Josef settled them warmly into a blanket. The two best friends were allowing the day to slide off their beings; worn, beaten, and bare.

"Do you remember the night we first met?" Melvin

said, smiling. The senior man's light, lighting the junior's.

"Always," Josef beamed. "I was crying."

Melvin laughed, recalling the flop of a teen. "You, sir, were bawling."

"Was it like a girl?" Josef fussed with animation.

"Indeed." Melvin laughed.

They sat enjoying the night as recalls were collected.

"That was the night I promised to always take care of you," Melvin offered to the night while Josef blinked his response as wet emotion.

"I never thought anyone could grant me the right to be… me," Josef replied with a smile as a tear dropped.

Melvin recalled the night four years ago when he was twenty, and little Josef was just fourteen.

***

Melvin couldn't tell where the woman in distress was. He scurried the backside of the stranger's barn, looking for the haunting wails.

"Oh!" Melvin was shocked by his newfound charge. "You're a boy."

Little Josef tried righting himself in the presence of the stranger. "You're English?"

Melvin chuckled, "Yes. You're male?"

Josef laughed and responded, "Apparently." He stood and curtsied, sending Melvin into a roar of laughter. He slowly collected himself, guffawing at the waif who seemed to recognize what he was to this world. Melvin appreciated the authenticity. He moved in to raise a cheer in the laddie.

"What are your troubles?" Melvin asked sincerely.

The boy was uncertain. Melvin continued. "I'm going to show you something if you promise not to tell anyone."

"Why would you do that?" the child wondered aloud.

"Because I trust you," Melvin affirmed. He then lit his moonbeam eyes, which dazzled and awed little Josef.

"How...?" the child sang, watching the release of the status quo, allowing for new possibilities; Melvin dappling them in delight, playing and gaining trust. They laughed and eventually landed close to one another. Melvin reached out to find Josef's shore, his far-off distant land where he walked alone.

"Tell me, what's wrong?" Melvin tried. "I want to help."

Josef righted his position, finding a twist in his neck. "I...," he began, trying to find his voice. "I play-act my entire life."

"What do you mean?" Melvin questioned.

"You see how I am now?" Melvin nodded. "This is me. This is how I am naturally, but...." Josef cut his eyes to a questioning tone.

"Go on...," Melvin pressed.

"Obviously, this isn't acceptable." He shrugged with a purse that he had stolen.

"It is unconventional," Melvin confirmed.

"Obviously, right? So I play act."

"Your entire life, you act as a character."

"Yes."

Melvin was awed at the weight of that commission. "Can I see?"

Josef righted himself into a brawnier version of himself. It was a masterclass in shape-shifting.

"Josef!" Melvin said in disbelief, and the boy continued his manly show. "How did you learn that?"

"What? To be someone else?" He shrugged. "I taught myself —had to. It was that or be killed." He then sunk into sadness. "I can only go back home as long as I'm willing to play the charade."

The caretaker in Melvin stepped in. "How about we find a few options for you."

"Truly?" Josef hoped.

"Yes. Truly. I will not rest until you are a free and happy...." Not sure landing on 'man' felt correct. He eventually said, *"person."*

***

Coming back to the moment, Melvin side hugged Josef, affirming, "Thank you. For everything. You really are my best friend."

Josef had his usual eyes for his senior as they shared the moment in the glow of familial love.

The following few days were spent in much the same routine, only Melvin taking more time with Johann to prepare him for the impending visitors the moment Samuel woke up. The small boy's ongoing cocoon was rebuilding his life force while blending with newfound fire. His internal warrior waking to a collapsed shell, a fight that would not break until the Mother Goddess's internal healing was complete. Things in this realm have to work in organic order.

Chapter 10

Thunderstruck

The week wore on to New Year's Eve's eve — and with the wind of the calendar days, Melvin could feel polarities intersecting. The stars this time of year checking their balances.

Melvin had just finished the morning's chores when he heard a deafening crash. It was coming from the front door. He dashed in its direction only to be stopped by Josef.

"It's the authorities," the junior panted as Melvin ran toward the intruders, only to be cut off by Felix.

"Father!" Felix stormed as the students gathered — the building's foyer once again becoming a scuttle of wits. Herr Meir seized Felix by the throat and threw him to the floor, cursing him with, "FAGGOT!" he screamed through tears.

Felix tried to regain himself as a new creature flew by him at velocity. It was Christian, and she arrived to the scene with fearlessness. "Can I help you?!" She charged the large man towering over his son. The father's disgust was bleeding from his eyes. With a rolling pin, Christian attacked, pushing and heaving him as if he was cattle, forcing him back, then back, then back again! Her tenacity was awe-inspiring.

"WAIT!" It was Felix from the floor. "I was speaking!" The gay-boy cursed back at his dad. Christian stepped aside, curious about the newfound care that Felix had found. Until now, he seemed to only care for himself.

"Father, I disown you," Felix said, side-swiping his mouth, checking for blood while recovering his feet. "We know what you and Mother were planning for my future...." He reached for his lover's hand and walked with the air of threats to face the situation. "I'm reclaiming what's mine and what was NEVER yours to give." Felix found exasperation and leveled, "Are you capable of understanding what love is?" An expectant tone hung in the air. "Is cutting into young people's flesh without their consent loving?"

"Herr Vaughn!" The Commander punctuated into the space. "Come with me. You are under arrest." Several police officers entered the foyer as Christian and Felix tried to block the exit. "Downstairs!" Herr Maier ordered as Melvin raced to beat the troops.

Reaching the basement first, Melvin swerved toward Herr Soliman, seated by his unconscious son. "We must protect the boy!" Melvin rushed, hearing the clatter in the stairwell behind him. He reached Samuel and turned to see one armed guard clock Herr Soliman's face with the blunt end of a gun. The force of it made an audible 'CRACK!' as he screamed in pain, grabbing for his face.

The sound of Herr Soliman's pain was a vibration that somehow found root in Samuel's primal way. It seemed to be a pang in the son's understanding from eons back, a stirring that cracked open his cocooning husk. He sat up and screamed of holy terror. Samuel screamed the scream of a child whose mind had just steeped for a week in things not understood.

"Johann!" Melvin screamed toward the stairs as the child immediately appeared and swung into the gymnasium, eyes lit to the darkest green before black. Melvin watched him fly into the space leveling up and gaining.

Johann then flattened the atoms in the room with the call. "Bumbgalla! Come," he summoned.

Melvin held the child and spun to see as he had feared. The elephant was now, indeed, visibly entering the room. In the dim gym, screams were unleashed as flicks of light bared witness to inhuman things. Chaos and elephant trumpets erupted. Flicker, Gorilla, flicker, scream… which was outdone by Bumbgalla's deafening roar in the enclosed cement room.

Embracing Samuel, Melvin ran for safety. He had hoped for more practice with Johann, but at least they knew the plan. The time was now. The teacher dove into Samuel's way, swimming deep into the boy's conscience. Melvin knew that once he extinguished the child's mind, the rest would also cease. Besides, he had jungle boy and his heavy, the silverback, babysitting the pachyderm —now, if he could shake the authorities.

He commutated levels without abandon, leveling himself to full unrestrained Wereclair bright. He needed this throttle of speed to carry out the plan. Melvin pulse-flexed into his upmost level, onboarding spells. "GO!" He flew with the moon's light, a mere streak in the dim hall. Silence Samuel. Done. He refocused. Ensure the children are safe. Done. He turned finally to the guards, dimming their lights to unconscious. "Done," Melvin confirmed to himself as he exhaled, returning to a more human expression.

"Get on what lights you can. And take out the trash," Melvin said, gently kicking one of the guards. He refocused to Herr Soliman. "Are you okay?" The senior man was bleeding from his skull. "Let's wait, then wake Samuel in a gentle, reassuring manner.

Glad he is conscious again. I merely put him into a differing vibration… to accommodate sleep.”

“Thank you. He’s awake then?” he asked as the two of them grabbing cloths to tend to the wound.

Melvin shoulder-checked a new normal, seeing a gorilla carry an unconscious man out of the room. “Yes, indeed. I was able to confirm the two seconds he was awake. He is ready. He will wake this time.”

The room finally quieted, and Melvin took Samuel in his arms and held him next to his father. “Here,” Melvin offered. Herr Soliman took his son, smiling with tears, while Melvin bandaged the father’s brow.

“My boy,” he confirmed to the universe.

Melvin tied the wrap, offering, “With your permission, I am going to begin.” Herr Soliman nodded. Melvin refocused on the child to wake him. He put his soothing energy into the boy and slowly began to rouse him.

“Samuel,” Melvin cheered quietly.

Eventually, the boy stirred and opened his eyes. “Pa.”

“Ja seun,” Herr Soliman cried.

Seeing that all was being restored in good order, Melvin gave them space.

CHAPTER 11

KNOCKING NEWS

The following day Josef burst into Melvin's office in his typical pink fashion. "Herr Vaughn! The Post!"

Melvin turned curious, "From my love? Let me... see...." His mind was already a wander reading the return address: Nikolai Tesla. It was indeed from him!

"Here," Josef bubbled, handing him scissors, a hammer, and a crowbar to get the nailed box open.

Melvin had never felt so gay. His joy button fired on all thrusters. "Come. Help me." The two of them wedged on metal bars that eeked and creaked hope. They finally beat the monster box, and Melvin paused to look at Josef. "What could it be?" Melvin's eyebrows danced.

"Get to it." Josef clapped. "Open it. I cannot stand it one more second!" His tone was in the register of bats.

Melvin cleared away the packing straw and took out a model of a building. He immediately knew what his love had done. He had brought their heart's ask to this plane so the universe could connect to its register. "Bravo," Melvin awed, turning the magic modeled before him. He rushed it to the credenza in his office to view it at eye level. Josef was a squeal of anticipation.

"Let me see!" Josef hurried.

Melvin placed it on the sideboard and stepped back to admire its mastery. Indeed it was everything they had discussed and hoped and wished. Melvin inspected it, showing Josef the rooms.

"Here is the main dining hall, which can be transformed into a theatre!" Melvin smiled. He moved to the next box around the courtyard. "This is the formal schooling and college. Over here are the living quarters."

"But...." Josef began.

"But why is it all encased in a giant glass crystal?" Melvin said, naming the obvious.

"Yes. I've never seen a building built inside a greenhouse before."

"We're not just building a school," Melvin named, "we're building a new way of life. A model. A sustainable way to live in concert with Mother Nature. To honor her and leave her better than we each found her. It all begins there," Melvin said. His internal sense of childhood wonder shined bright. His heart center was glowing into moonbeam tears. "It all begins there."

"I must get going to get lunch ready for the students. It is an architectural marvel," Josef said as he left the room.

Melvin moved to the wood box to see if it housed a note. It did.

Melvin, my love,

The medical credential for you will arrive soon. Is the program to unnaturally alter young boys still underway? I hope I am in time, and I hope you receive this Christmas present by the day. Post has been extremely slow of late. I do not understand folks who take employment with no lovejoy. They only seek to muddy the otherwise good working industry, built by people who care about such things.

My employment is again shifting, and I have seen my final day at The Edison Machine Works. It seems that people amuse themselves with here include offering large sums of money as commission, only to find out there was no such deal. It bothers me endlessly how immature many of my constituents are here. They conduct themselves in a manner that is brash and not in accordance with the ways of a gentleman.

The last of the financing for the school in upstate New York has been inked. So come spring, we will be moving earth on the additions.

Keep me posted on the students. Please assure me that you have everything under control. Honestly, Mel, most people would not believe some of the situations in which you find yourself. I cannot wait to meet them all, menagerie included. Small gifts for the students are packaged under a removable floor in the box. I didn't care for the idea of them clanging about and breaking our magic dreamhouse—the place where all are encouraged to be as they are.

I love you, Melvin. I apologize if I have not said that enough in your presence, but I see it now. I see how precious our time is together. That's all there is. That's all that matters—time and us.

With all that I am.

Very Truly Yours,

Nikolai

Melvin grabbed a pen to respond.

Dearest Nikolai,

Here it is, December 30th, and today has arrived with my heart alight. My love, the things you conjure are nothing short of mastery, and the arrival of your model handiwork is indeed impressive.

My junior Josef was here when it arrived, and I was able to give him the basic outline but didn't yet relay the other parts of the structure until you have confirmed that we can pull it off. It indeed will be a feat of engineering. My heart races with visions of the possibilities. A forever rainbow on Rainbow Lake, New York.

As for the students, thank you for the many gifts. I will see they receive them.

Samuel is recovering well. However, we're still unclear how 'Det store vesenet,' The Great Becoming, will unfold within him. It shall be interesting indeed as this child is so young. He is being leveled up six years earlier than

He put down his pen, exhaling knots, the weight of the daily demands crashing in on him. Seeking answers, Melvin moved to face himself in the mirror. His reflection was again intolerable, its glow of youth and innocence mocking his true nature. However, he found in this moment, he couldn't name it. He could no longer pinpoint who and what he was. It all simply seemed insurmountable and unmoored.

Melvin felt his mind slip. Tears began rolling down his face. His exhaustion and uncertainty were becoming too much.

"How am I to do this when I fake every move and know nothing?" he asked of his reflection. "I have only the direction of my guides, nothing else." He moved to place his back on the wall, and slowly lowering himself to the floor, he repeated, "Nothing else." He erupted in tears, cratered on the floor, too aware of the emptiness of his life without Nikolai.

Moving to a more seated position, Melvin's eye caught the register. The book that now contained one hundred and sixty-seven names of young men who were scheduled to be surgically separated from their minds. Every time he had to touch that book, his insides hit themselves into a stammer that Melvin thought might be his undoing. *I have to be strong,* he told himself, wiping at tears. Melvin repositioned against the wall again to arrest his nonsense, berating himself for allowing precious seconds to be wasted on such folly.

"Damn," he said aloud, shaking himself into a new tone. Trying to pull it together, Melvin tethered to a good memory, and a smile came across his way, carried by the vibrations he was flicking at that contained the memory of the night they conceived of the living rainbow on Rainbow Lake, New York.

Chapter 12

Midnight Train

Melvin recalled their many nights of unchecked passion and how it would unfold each night into naming dreams.

***

"Beloved," Nikolai said, unwinding himself from Melvin's grasp. The two of them came face to face, enjoying the warmth of their bodies pressing flesh. Melvin smiled, still breathing heavily from their nightly exchange of them. "I have come up with a vision."

"Come up with a vision or received a vision?" Melvin's comment immediately arrested the professor's train of thought.

"Ha," Nikolai joyed. "You are something else. You know that?"

"Indeed," Melvin said, catching cold truth. "I'm probably not the most normal mate you might have."

The senior man brushed at blonde curls, then exhaled, saying, "And for that, I am blessed." He kissed Melvin, holding him in a manner that conveyed his passion and spirit. Nikolai's grip expressed vows as he climbed onto his love. "We shall make it. We will. We must."

The two men stared into possibilities, eyeing and angling for hope. "But how can our place for bi-gendered and queer individuals even exist? Anywhere we go, we shall be discovered and jailed. In case you haven't noticed, the expression of ourselves is illegal."

Nikolai slowed to get clear. "For now."

"For now? How about forever!"

"You really have no hope."

"Have you met our fellow humans?" Melvin said flatly — a comment that made the teacher laugh. "They, I assure you, are terrible."

"They are as they are, and they make the rules. But aren't we smart enough to...," Nikolai reached at his truest meaning, "...to work within the system, until we can work without it."

"You believe we can make that and not be arrested? They will immediately shut down any school for effeminate boys, for to state that we exist is heresy."

"I have been working on something," Nikolai said in a hushed tone. "A way to disguise our presence."

This was news to Melvin. "What? What kind of disguise?"

"Are you familiar with the term cloaking?"

Melvin ran the term through his photographic memory of the dictionary he once read.

"Cloak: noun," he said aloud. "A loose outer garment, as a cape or coat. Oh, nice!" Melvin bounced. "Show me!"

Nikolai laughed and collapsed into Melvin, their naked bodies enjoying being what they were to each other in this abandoned place. "No. Not a cloak, but cloaking, as in to hide or obfuscate."

Nikolai grabbed Melvin's hand and sprung out of bed. "Come!" They ran to the door, where Nikolai grabbed two blankets, and they continued their naked streak out into the night, laughing. "Here!" Nikolai said, throwing a blanket out on the grass under the moon. Melvin lept onto it and threw the other blanket onto himself.

A minute later, Nikolai returned with a curious expression and some strange-looking objects.

"Have you heard of sympathetic resonance?"

Melvin turned a thought. "I have not."

"Excellent. It's not ready to show my constituents, but it's held my imaginings for a while now. Hold this, like this." He handed Melvin a solid metal object in the shape of a 'y'. He held it as instructed.

"It's called a tuning fork."

Melvin turned it over, inspecting the thing. "Well, it's very nice." He said politely, unsure of what might happen next.

"Don't move yours and don't touch the upper part; just the bottom holder." Nikolai began slowly striking the one he was holding with a mallet. It started to sing!

"That's beautiful. So it's a musical thing?" The hum of its ring was gaining in volume and resonance.

"Watch!" Nikolai awed. He then repeatedly struck his fork while slowly backing away from Melvin, seated on the ground. The fork's vibrational resonance was getting louder and louder until the entire backyard rang of its song. The naked men laughed, the moment under the moon stirring a summer night's delight.

However, Melvin wouldn't have believed what happened next if he hadn't heard it with his own ears and felt it with his own hand. Nikolai was next to the house when he dropped his tuning fork into a bucket, and as the water met the thing, it immediately silenced it — however, it didn't arrest the song, which continued to sing out into the night air. It made no sense how the thing could continue to resound from beyond its vibrational death.

Melvin next realized the sound was now, in fact, coming from the fork in his hand. "What?" Melvin laughed into the night as Nikolai ran naked toward him.

"Isn't it simply impossible?"

"Indeed. How is this working? What is this?"

Nikolai pushed himself on top of Melvin, took the thing into his hand, and then pulled Melvin to face him as they both lay on their sides. "Somehow, when I strike one, the other catches the song."

"Truly?"

"Sympathetic resonance. It's a harmonic musical phenomenon that defies understanding; when one begins its song, others can't help but join. Its influence is, captivating and empowering in ways we can't even understand. It's all energy and vibration."

"The language in light," Melvin confirmed to the man who first introduced such a concept to his mind. The truth of it lay bare what Melvin always felt and somehow understood. It was the information in the unseen. It was the knowing he could gain from the briefest encounter with a solitary sunbeam.

"Yes!" Nikolai laughed. "You remember!"

"How could I forget!" Melvin screamed, escalating the gaiety of the moment. "That was the first night we officially met."

Nikolai stood and dashed back toward the house. "Hold on...," he said over his shoulder, only to reappear a moment later carrying a bottle of wine, a corkscrew, and glasses. He stood naked with an expression of trouble, then confirmed, "Indeed it was." He sat and began the winding of screws. "A night I shall not soon forget."

Melvin laughed. "I was so nervous meeting you."

Nikolai popped the cork saying, "You were adorable." He poured two glasses and then offered one. "Still are."

To avoid the crush of the blush with his cheeks finding fire, Melvin offered, "So why the tuning fork experiment? Why did you want to show me that?"

"There are things we cannot see that will change our world."

Melvin lit his eyes lightly. "Yes." He laughed. "We both understand this."

"So why do you have no hope, beloved? We live in a magical time on a magical planet where anything is possible." He pointed to the stars. "I am working on something that will veil our works and allow us to exist without interference. We shall be amongst them without their knowledge."

"How do you know?" The comment visibly deflated the senior who Melvin knew was doing his best to buoy hope.

"Alright. It isn't yet finished, but perhaps you might understand." He leaped up again and ran naked into the garden shed. He returned with a pane of glass, a garden hose, and a lit lightbulb on a long cord.

"Hold this," the professor instructed.

"Now what?" Melvin laughed, taking the framed glass, still seated under the stars.

"Get up. You're going to get wet." Nikolai cranked at the spigot and then sprayed a tease of water at the junior, making him run and squeal.

"Don't!" he laugh-complained while smiling. The midnight naked frolic made them both feel alive.

"Hold the glass in front of you." Melvin did as instructed. "We can see each other fine, correct?"

"Yes. No problem. I see you fine."

"Don't move." Nikolai then shackled the hose with a metal coupling that forced the stream into a mist. Finally, he sent the gentle spray between them. "How about now? Can you see me okay?"

"Indeed. No problem — but I don't understand the point of the exercise." Nikolai dropped the hose and ran back into the house, then returned with a human dummy, a chair, twine, and a music stand.

"Now what?!" Melvin yelled into the night, delighted with the continued show taking place. Nikolai laughed and rushed around the space, replacing Melvin with the dummy doll, then adjusting the window atop the music stand with the twine, its pane standing as a barrier of glass.

"Come," Nikolai joyed as the last of the experiment was set. Melvin moved into Nikolai's space, looking down the barrel of the water hose teaming with a fine spray. "Watch!"

Melvin put his naked body behind his love and watched over his shoulder as the unthinkable and unreal became understood. "That's us there." He pointed to the mannequin behind the window. "In the school."

"Okay...?" Melvin said, questioning.

"Hold the hose like this." Melvin did so as Nikolai took up the electrically lit bulb on a cord, then boxed it into focus, creating a stream of concentrated light. "Watch as I pass the light over the water mist."

As the senior poured the streams of light and water together, they met, creating a massive bloom of a rainbow into the night sky.

"A rainbow!" Melvin yelled with excitement.

"Not just a rainbow… a disguise. Can you see us in the school behind the glass?" Melvin checked the experiment.

"Indeed, I cannot. I only see fine mist and rainbows." They smiled, understanding that the magic they were creating was a thing spoken in the language in light.

"A shield of hope, beloved. They shall not find us. We will be safe." Then, with the flick of a wrist holding the hose, Nikolai threw a heart-shaped rainbow into the night's sky. "I promise."

Melvin heard a knock at the door, bringing him back to the present moment.

"Yes?" he inquired.

"Herr. Class beings in five minutes," Josef said from behind the door.

"Thank you, Josef." He began to ready himself for the morning's exercise.

CHAPTER 13

FENCING THE FIRMAMENT

"Students!" Melvin began his pace by addressing the young people. "Tonight is New Year's Eve!" Cheers were unleashed. "And we want to welcome our newest student to the class." Everyone turned to cheer on Samuel, whose first day of class was observed from his father's lap. The boy smiled and moved his gaze to the floor, his father rubbing his shoulders with encouragement.

"To begin…," the teacher said, snapping their attention back. "Let's share with Samuel the work we've been doing. We've spent much time understanding what's within us… because why?" Melvin searched the students for answers.

"Because what we have… internally, is what we have to give," Matteo proffered.

"Indeed!" Melvin cheered. "We have learned what you have to give. Haven't we?" The teacher smiled. "You have spoken often of this, so Matteo, tell us of your totem and calling this lifetime. What do you have to give? Show Samuel your work."

The fifteen-year-old then left his chair and went over to Samuel, asking. "What do you like?"

Samuel looked to his father, who encouraged him off his lap.

"Go on," Herr Soliman suggested.

"I like music," Samuel finally said quietly.

"Do you now?!" Matteo clapped. "How wonderful." The elder student then checked with the teacher, who nodded encouragement. He was doing it perfectly.

Samuel cracked into a smile as Matteo grabbed for his arm. They walked holding hands to the middle of the group, where Matteo sat on the floor, legs crossed. "Come."

Samuel sat in the boy's lap, cautiously trusting.

Matteo continued, "I like books and learning."

"Like Robin Hood?!" the boy pepped.

"Yes!" Matteo cheered. "Excellent — and from what I hear, you have quite the spirit animal. Imagine the adventures. Just like in Robin Hood!" The two boys laughed with abandon, like they were having a private moment, just the two of them. Melvin beamed with pride at Matteo's natural ability to teach. It was as if curiosity somehow translated to betterment and affirmation. The tie was clear.

"Where can we go?" Samuel said.

"What? On adventure?"

"Yes," Samuel bubbled.

"Oh, we go lots of places and see lots of things. Your guide is an elephant, is it not?"

Samuel shrugged a bit, unsure. A move that piqued the teacher's interest. Many questions were forming, but for now, Melvin observed.

Matteo continued, "My spirit guide is an octopus!"

Samuel laughed and squished his face, making wriggly motions of mimicry.

The teacher stepped in, "Please tell us of your totem for this work."

The student exhaled, readying his mind to speak his truth. "My totem arrived as an alien world. I didn't know where I was, and I couldn't tell if I was underwater or if there was air. It was not of anything I understood."

"Was there anything else? An object, or being or understanding?"

Matteo looked to Samuel on his lap as if he were telling a mighty tale. "There was an opening, like a hallway."

"Really?" The little boy was awed.

"Yes."

Melvin prompted more, saying, "And what does that mean to you? What's the gift you have for Samuel and the class? What does your totem say you have to give?"

"Adventure!" Matteo cheered, making Samuel join in the game. "And action!" The young boy caught the giggles as Matteo chased the dream. "We can go great distances and learn weird things." The room laughed.

Matteo chased on to finish his truth-telling. "I guess I have…," he pondered the words, "willingness, and a mind that seems discontent with the holes in the answers."

Hearing this, Melvin clapped, thinking that was an amazing way to describe his truth. Matteo was indeed a child who was discontent with the holes in the answers. Bravo kid. Well done.

"Excellent." Melvin then turned his attention to the lovers who were, as always, intertwined. "Boys. Please. Jakob — Captain Hummingbird." The students laughed. "Tell Samuel and us what you have to give in this work. What was your totem?"

"Hi." The gay boy flounced, making his way over to tiny Samuel. "Jakob. Nice to… well…." He redirected to the other students while standing next to Samuel, who was on the floor. "My boyfriend

Felix and I?" He hid a wave to his love. "We both have birds. Yes. His is a pea-cock." He said, hitting the cock part unnecessarily hard.

"Jakob. Address Samuel. Cut the crap."

"Fine." Jakob turned to face the boy. "Anyhow, Felix and I..."

"Enough." Melvin stopped the class. "Apparently, what you have to give on this day is chit-chat about your relationship. Is that what you think Samuel needs?"

Jakob deflated and got real. "No."

"You have about thirty seconds to get this right, or we are moving on."

Jakob sat on the floor next to Samuel, then turned to look at him. "My guide is a blue, green, and purple hummingbird." The room slowed its energy, waiting to see what might be offered next. "And my totem for this work was a long white flower. Not sure, but I felt like it could talk to me."

Samuel's eyes went wide. "Really?" The boy edged toward the teen.

"Yes."

"You can do that?"

Jakob looked to his teacher, uncertain of the path forward. Melvin stepped in.

"We are all learning many new things. It sounds like the plant nation wanted to communicate with you?"

"I'm not sure." Jakob shrugged.

"Excellent. Thank you." He turned to the oldest student in the pack. "Felix. You're up. What do you have to give Samuel this New Year's Eve?"

The strapping lad ambled center stage as Jakob worked his way back to his chair. "Okay, kid," Felix said, his pointed fingers miming guns. "My guide is a peacock, as Jakob mentioned, and my totem for this work was found as a gift an unnamed stranger gave me. Someone I could feel but not see. They gave me a set of Japanese throwing knives, kyoketsu-shoge. The type with the short hook on the blade that's attached to a long leather rope and a ring at the end."

"For throwing?!" Samuel asked in total disbelief.

"Yes," Felix answered flatly. "Anything else?" He eventually asked the teacher.

Melvin was deflated, unimpressed by the minimum amount of work being offered.

"If you're done," Melvin answered. "I'm done. How about that?"

The handsome young man gave a smart-ass bow and reseated himself amongst Jakob's appendages.

The balance of the morning wore on as all the students, even Josef, brought before Samuel their gifts. The class worked through incantations and declarations. They covered how to declare it, to make it so, and how never is nothing happening. Melvin then closed for the morning, demonstrating how energy follows the path of intention.

"Class dismissed," Melvin finally yelled as the students immediately flurried into action. "You have the day, but dinner at 6:00 and then our party tonight starts at 8:00 PM. Work on your wears! Your finest that also pays homage to your guide."

Josef clapped with excitement, adding, "I'll have my sewing notions and things in the dining room if anyone needs help." With that, the room fell back to silence, leaving only Melvin, Herr Soliman, and Samuel.

"May we speak alone?" Melvin offered.

Herr Soliman understood that the moment had come. "Let me get Samuel situated upstairs, perhaps with Matteo."

"I'll be in my office," Melvin said, heading for the stairs.

CHAPTER 14

ENTRAPMENT

Melvin was reading the paper when Herr Soliman presented himself. "Please, sit," Melvin indicated. Once righted, he continued. "I do not sense much transference of magic energy in your child. Some, yes… but not knowing him before the transference, I'm having difficulty getting a read."

Herr Soliman thought about what was just said. "He seems, perhaps, more alive, if that's possible."

Hearing this, Melvin was thrown into a clap. "Really?! You can tell a difference?"

"Some. Like you said."

Melvin knew it was time to ask the tough question. "I mean no assumptions by this question, and I only ask for research purposes; to help us better understand the trap and how it affects those who have it awakened within them."

"I understand. Go on."

"Does Samuel have effeminate traits?"

Herr Soliman's face found a twist as he managed, "He's eight."

To which Melvin fired back, "Johann and the twins are twelve. Trust me! You know."

The room found its way to the tone of a laugh as Herr Soliman let down his guard. "Not that I'm aware of."

"I was sensing the same. Thank you for answering honestly." Melvin headed for the stairs. "Shall we? It's already proving to be a magical day."

Moving down the main floor hall, Melvin noticed a note under the front door. He retrieved it, noting it was addressed to Felix. He went in search of the young man.

"Felix!" he yelled up the stairs chasing his voice. "Felix!" The student appeared.

"Yes?"

"A note." Melvin waved the letter. "Come. My office. Now." They ran the halls with questions.

"Sit," Melvin directed, closing the door behind them. "Please open it so we can discuss. Are you okay with the course of action? I think it is best, even though this is your letter. There are many things and lives to consider."

"I understand," Felix said as he opened the envelope. He read aloud, "Felix, please come home. We do not understand your choices but still want you here. There is much at stake for your future. In time you will understand. Please send word as to your decision. All I ask, in exchange for all I have given you as my son, is that if you decide to stay with those people, you meet me in person one last time. I at least deserve that. An opportunity to say goodbye in person —then, it's signed," Felix pointed to the papered notions. "Your father."

Felix sat back and exhaled, staring into the ceiling's universe.

"How does that make you feel?" Melvin asked.

The young man thought about it as his face turned the color of sadness. "They gave me everything. They wanted me as a pawn...." He wiped a tear. "For their Empire. But I'm not...." His face searched for the right word, landing on, "that." He continued the verbal wander. "I love Jakob. I never knew this feeling before. He makes me feel so alive and like I have purpose."

Melvin smiled, cheering on the ownership of the youth's heart. "What do you wish to do? How do you want to respond to the note?"

"I want out. I want to end it. We both know what they were planning for my future. I owe him nothing, but I would like closure for myself. Would it be okay if that meeting took place here?"

Melvin thought about it. He noted that they already knew the address, so that was one check in the pro column, plus they did have several other options within the walls under their control.

"Excellent idea. What feels right to you. How would you like for this to unfold?"

"Is it foolish of me to give him one last chance? I don't know, but I still hope that if he sees my friends and my relationship, how much in love we are, and how happy Jakob makes me, well…." The junior didn't finish the sentence, but Melvin well understood.

"Very good then. Send word to invite him to our festivity. We shall welcome him with open arms," Melvin assured. "Go. Send word."

CHAPTER 15

INVISIBLE ORCHESTRATIONS

It was well past the dinner hour as the students began to dress for the evening's festivities. Josef screamed and ran after last-minute adjustments. The caterwauling of excitement was deafening.

"Matteo!" Josef yelled. "Damn it…," he said, scattering himself around the space. "And you?" he said as a song to the teacher. "So nice you themed the party after something you can't participate in."

"True," Melvin agreed. "But what I lack in spirit animal guide, I make up for in other ways." His headlamps hit a few blinking pulses.

"You are a ridiculous person," Josef confirmed to his boss's face, then went on down the hall like he owned the place.

"Okay! Everyone to the rooftop!" Melvin said with good cheer. "Party begins in ten minutes."

The building found a flurry of gaiety as the twins worked with Matteo on the electricity. They even managed to light a few bulbs! Christian found her fiddle and lit the air with joy while teenagers screamed and laughed in their schoolyard way.

Arriving into the night air, "Excellent!" Melvin encouraged Jakob, who was already dancing to the fiddle's jig. He noted Matteo and the twins must be still fussing with the electricity in the basement when he found Josef in a corner by the rooftop stairs. He headed over to pep-step his charge. "Tuckered out, lad?" He jigged and then sat next to Josef.

"That's Miss to you, but yes," he deflated. "I'm about spent."

"You always have had endless energy." At that moment, the rooftop hushed as Felix entered with his father.

"Everyone," Felix beamed. "This is my dad." The air was filled with promise as Melvin stood and then strode to greet the man. However, as he approached, he was stopped by a large book being presented into the space between them. Herr Maier wielded the sacred text of his faith Spectre's Shadow: Blood Lust. It's outer casing naming the Norweigein conjuring alchemies spekterets skygge: Blod lyst. Felix's father shoved his son out of his space, then opened the tome and began chanting one of the darkest spells in the book: Hvit død, or white death.

"Forfedre! Forfedre!" Herr Maier began shouting to the heavens, making everyone come to a halt. They watched it play out. Herr Maier continued his divination. "Kom med døden! Kom forfedre!"

Melvin couldn't help but start to laugh. What did this fool think he was going to do? Cast advanced magic when he's never done any of the entry-level work? He didn't even have the eyes yet to see where love existed, let alone adopt the internal workings of cross-grid energy work. No one who spews hate has access to the depths of honesty required for evolved work. The man was not a threat, and it was confusing to all who watched. Others began to enjoy the show as Felix rushed to interrupt.

"Father!" Felix screamed. "Enough. Are you seeking to harm others?"

Herr Maier then dropped the book and drew a gun. He focused it squarely on Felix, rendering the night silent. "Why?!" he leveled as a crime against his son. "We wanted to give you everything," he seethed. "And you threw it in the garbage!" he yelled. Everyone was backing away from the pistol when Herr Soliman charged, rushing low with all his might. Herr Maier turned quickly and shot him in the head, his body crashing as a pile of bones to the floor. People screamed into the night air.

"Abomination," Herr Maier said in a tone that made clear the resonance of hate that that word represents, for to charge any group with such a crime would be to seal their tortured fates.

Herr Maier trained his gun back on Felix, backing him toward the corner of the roof. "You disgust me. You broke your mother's heart. Just tell me why?"

"Can't you see that Jakob… and my friends," he shimmied with desperation, crying, "make me happy? Why can't you see what's plainly there? I'll never understand it."

"Good-bye, son." As Herr Maier squeezed the trigger, Felix's true love appeared.

Out of nowhere, Jakob lunged at his boyfriend to push him out of the way, desperate to save him.

Melvin watched in slow motion as Jakob slammed into Felix, the bullet piercing the younger lover's skull, erupting in a pink mist. Melvin saw Jakob's last breath of life. The light went out, the bullet killing him instantly.

As Jakob's dead body fell to the floor, chaos erupted. Felix screamed with the torment of a fractured mind. His face hit an inert expression of horror that failed to move. Melvin lunged for Herr Maier, doing his best to capture the gun, and as his fingers found metal, a massive blow struck from behind.

The world slowed as Melvin went into hyperdrive to assess what was happening. It was Christian. She steamrolled into Herr Maier, knocking them off balance. Christian slammed into them again with even greater force, throwing them back to the roof's edge.

In slow motion, Melvin witnessed his mother arrive from the heavens as Felix's trap was sprung, exploding energy a mile high, his body beginning to lift into mid-air.

Johann was already a flail of dark green as Bumbgalla entered the space. The two of them flew into action to arrest the danger.

Melvin hit hyper-drive again, slowing the world yet more.

It was slow-motion chaos and terror. Felix's body exploded above the rooftops in the air. His body was ripped from his earthly form, and a giant shrieking bird of blue and green terror whipped the air into a frenzy. It was torrents of cosmic energy erupting from the mind of a man whose love was just destroyed by those who claim to love him the most, a mind-fuck so categorically complete that no human child could survive. He screamed in agony and horror as his body continued to be dismembered from its lies.

Melvin sped on as a whirl of an enraged elephant blasted past Josef, who lunged for Samuel. The child was unmoving and was in shock. Melvin feared for the building's stability as he witnessed Christian heave Herr Maier off the edge of the building. The man grabbed mid-flail, attaching himself to her neck scarf.

Melvin bolted for her but failed to cross the space in time. He watched them breach the crest and fall beyond the building's horizon. Melvin screaming full throttle, rushed with all he had to give, bargaining with others in the beyond.

Reaching the roof's edge, Melvin looked down, and as he left the rim of solidity, hitting mid-air, he witnessed something unexpected. What he witnessed was holy. What he witnessed was divine. What he witnessed he would never forget.

In Melvin's mid-air time-bent hyper-warp mind, he recorded a woman of all genders falling in slow motion toward her death, reclaiming her rightful place in glory. Christian's scream cracked her open to source energy itself that blasted to the heavens unrestrained. The Divine Feminine, Melvin's Mother filled the balance of the space, moving from Felix's awakening to Christian's. Melvin watched his mother, who had no words for them because no lower work was being done on this day, release Christian's lie. The lie of her lower self and the lie that held the world's evolution back.

Det store vesenet, The Great Becoming, unleashed Christian's truest self, the part that is unwounded and unwoundable. Melvin watched Christian step into her loving power, leveling up in consciousness. A thing truly from the divine attached to her as corded cables of lightning shackling her as shimmering electricity that yoked her, then yoked her again. Chains of light found their way into her being. She crumbled mid-air with the restraints. The bolts of lightning seeking to unearth truths and shackle-back lies.

As the trap within Christian was finally sprung, an explosive radiant blue light that owned all consciousness became omnipresent, its light blinding. A beacon that shone to the heavens, a portal to Athena herself.

Time stopped.

Melvin looked around. Everything was frozen. Time had indeed frozen. He heard his name, but not his English name.

"Måne."

Hearing this, Melvin's heart thundered. He turned in the voice's direction. "Yes?"

"You asked what you need to know."

"Yes," he confirmed.

"There's something we need to show you," the Angel Nation said.

A blinking white light appeared as a doorway where Christian's heart beat. Melvin took a breath, steadying himself, knowing that fear is an illusion. The portal that was marked as Christian was growing and enveloping.

Melvin knew he had done the work and unpacked it all down to its barest nubs —and in that level of truth, where the fear option is no more, the answer easily presented itself.

"Love is all there is." He awed, stepping forward through the blinking white portal, trusting the intelligence of the universe that radiates with one thing only.

The final thing Melvin remembered was stepping into the radiant Christian light, his eyes connecting with the still falling Herr Maier

— the one who was incapable of seeing love, where it exists; the one who spewed hate as righteousness. The one who applauded fascism as righteousness.

Falling through the blinking portal into the Angel Nation's realm, he cut to steel to address all that was Christian and all that was Herr Maier. He leveled his charge, never more sure of his wrath. His final words he spat in his oppressor's face.

"This ends with me."

And with that, the world exploded into a million colors and ferried Melvin away.

A Note from the Author

If you enjoyed reading *Where the Warrior Lives*, please leave a review on Amazon. I read every review, and they help new readers discover my books.

Handsome Devils and *An Army Awakens,* books one and two in *The Language in Light book* series, are available on Amazon in both Kindle and print versions. To order your copies or leave reviews of those books, visit tinyurl.com/handsomedevils or tinyurl.com/anarmyawakens

Christian's Rapture, book four in *The Language in Light* series, is coming soon!

I also invite you to check out my YouTube channel, where I cover many of the topics discussed in *The Language in Light* book series, as well as topics ranging from shamanism to manifesting and evolving in this ever-expanding reality in which we exist. Visit and subscribe at YouTube.com/DaleAllenRowse

For more information, visit www.DaleAllenRowse.com.

About the Author

Dale Allen-Rowse always knew he was a creator and a storyteller. However, it wasn't until Celine Dion hired him as an original cast member for her show 'A New Day' that he understood his calling. During the almost year-long creation of Celine's Las Vegas show, Dale's vision for storytelling, narrative, and fantasy emerged. He worked for three years under the direction of

Dion's director, Franco Dragone, the creative genius behind many of the Cirque de Soleil shows. From that relationship, Dale discovered his voice.

In 2005, Dale left Celine's employment, ending an eighteen-year professional theatre performing career to pursue a new life in real estate. Within three years of becoming a real estate agent, Dale was awarded top honors for individual sales volume for RE/MAX and opened a brokerage firm.

After a twenty-year career as an agent and real estate coach, Dale is adding new passions to his interests, including his spiritual life as a shamanic practitioner and student of core shamanism. With the publishing of Handsome Devils, Dale realizes a lifelong dream of becoming an author who seeks to challenge the status quo through modern-day fables that study and dissect energy work.

Dale channels his books using 'Automatic Writing,' which he discusses on YouTube.com/DaleAllenRowse channel — as well as many of the topics covered in his books, such as personal evolution, spiritual energy work, core shamanism, manifesting, and evolving. Plus, his talks are set to a disco beat, and that's not nothing.

Dale and his husband John live on a five-acre ranch in Mountain Center, California. They currently have five dogs with a miniature donkey possibly in their future. Other things that keep Dale occupied are his quilts — you can see his work online as the Quilting Cowboy — and his day job as a real estate sales educator and coach.

www.ingramcontent.com/pod-product-compliance
Lightning Source LLC
Chambersburg PA
CBHW031415310726
48971CB00003B/872